D is for Danger...

Suddenly a scream burst from the castle behind them.

Dink nearly dropped his end of the picnic basket. The skin on his arms erupted into a thousand goose bumps.

The kids looked at each other, wide-eyed.

Wallis glanced back and grinned. "Dink, Josh, Ruth Rose, allow me to introduce...the ghost of Emory Scott!"

The A to Z Mysteries™ series!

The Absent Author

The Bald Bandit

The Canary Caper

The Deadly Dungeon

For Emily and Zach
–R.R.

To Emily, for being a great Ruth Rose
–J.S.G.

ISBN 0-590-81922-4

Published by Scholastic Inc., 555 Broadway, New York, NY 10012,
by arrangement with Random House, Inc.
A TO Z MYSTERIES is a trademark of Random House, Inc.
SCHOLASTIC and associated logos are trademarks and/or registered
trademarks of Scholastic Inc.

12 11 10 9 8 7 6   1 2 3 4/0

Printed in the U.S.A.   40

First Scholastic printing, January 1999

A to Z Mysteries™

The Deadly Dungeon

by Ron Roy

illustrated by
John Steven Gurney

SCHOLASTIC INC.
New York Toronto London Auckland Sydney
Mexico City New Delhi Hong Kong

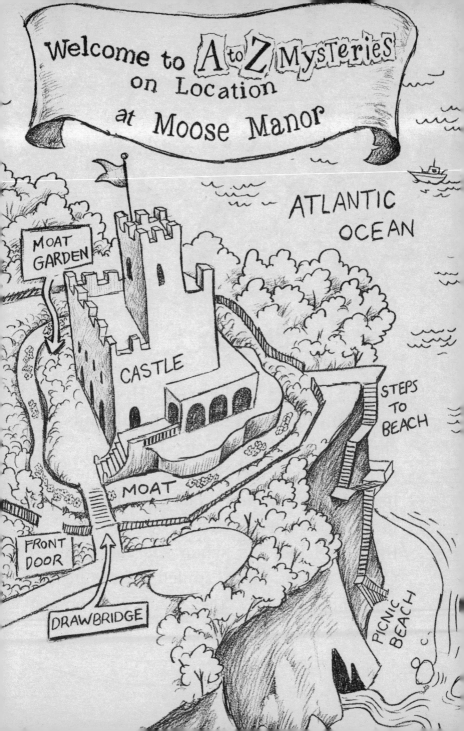

Chapter 1

Dink squirmed in his seat. He, Josh, and Ruth Rose had been riding the bus since seven that morning.

They were on their way to Maine to visit their friend Wallis Wallace, a famous mystery writer. The three of them had met her when she came to Green Lawn. Dink smiled when he remembered how they had rescued Wallis from a "kidnapper."

Dink glanced over at Josh, asleep in his seat. His sketch pad was open on his lap.

Behind Josh, Ruth Rose was looking at a map. She liked to dress in one color. Today it was green, from her T-shirt to her high-tops.

Dink moved into the seat next to Ruth Rose. "Where are we?" he asked.

"Almost there." She pointed to Belfast, Maine, on her map. "We just passed a Welcome to Belfast sign."

Dink nodded. That was where Wallis was picking them up.

Ruth Rose tucked her map into her pack. "I'm so excited!" she said. "Do you think her castle has a moat and a dungeon?"

"I just hope it has food," Dink said. "I'm starving!"

Josh's head popped up in front of them. "Me too! Are we there yet?"

Just then the bus driver called out, "Belfast!"

"All right!" Josh said, leaping into the aisle.

The bus stopped in front of a small gray-shingled building. Through the window, Dink could see the water.

"Do you see Wallis?" Ruth Rose asked.

Dink grabbed his pack. "No, but let's get off. I think I'm allergic to buses!"

The kids headed for the front. They followed an elderly couple down the steps.

They were squinting into the blinding sunlight when they heard someone say, "Hi, kids!" A tall man with curly blond hair was walking toward them. His face was tanned and smiling.

"I remember you. You're Wallis's brother!" Ruth Rose said.

"Call me Walker, okay?" said the

man. "Wallis is buying groceries, so she asked me to get you."

Walker Wallace picked up Dink's pack. It clunked heavily against his leg.

"What's in here, your rock collection?" he asked.

Dink grinned. "Books. My mom said it rains a lot in Maine, so I came prepared."

Walker laughed. "We've planned perfect weather for you guys. Sun every day! Come on, that's my Jeep over there."

Walker's dusty brown Jeep had no top. The leather seats were worn and split in places.

He swept a pair of boots and a tool belt onto the floor, making room in the backseat. "Pile in!"

The boys climbed into the back. Ruth Rose sat next to Walker. "How far is the castle?" she asked.

"Not far." Walker pointed. "About a mile past those trees."

He drove up the coast. "You guys hungry? Sis is buying everything in the store for you."

"I'm *always* hungry," Josh said, leaning back and crossing his legs. He took a deep breath of the ocean air. "What a smell!"

"I'll say," Dink said. "Get your smelly foot out of my face!"

"It's not smelly," Josh said, wiggling his sneaker under Dink's nose.

"What's this?" Dink plucked a bright green feather off the sole of Josh's sneaker.

Josh shrugged. "I must've picked it up on the bus."

Dink slipped the feather into his pocket.

"There's Moose Manor!" Walker called. He pointed through the trees.

Dink stared at the tall castle. It was built of huge gray stones. Its small dark windows looked like watching eyes. An iron fence surrounded the building.

"Cool," Dink said softly.

"Look, guys, a moat!" Ruth Rose said.

"And a drawbridge!" cried Josh.

Walker pulled up in front of the gate. The kids hopped out with their packs.

"I have to get back to my boat," Walker said. "Sis should be here soon. Have fun!" He waved and sped back through the trees.

Up close, the castle towered over the kids. The battlements on top reminded Dink of giant's teeth.

Josh pushed the gate, and it creaked open. They peered down into the moat. Ruth Rose let out a laugh. "Look, guys!"

The bottom of the empty moat was planted with flowers!

"Hey, guys!" Josh called. "Check this out!" He had crossed the drawbridge and was standing in front of an enormous wooden door. He tugged on the handle, but the door wouldn't budge. "How the heck does Wallis get in?"

Just then Dink heard a car. A red Volkswagen convertible zoomed up to the gate. The horn tooted, and a hand waved wildly.

"It's Wallis!" shouted Dink.

Chapter 2

"Welcome!" Wallis yelled.

She looked the same as Dink remembered: happy smile, curly brown hair, mischievous eyes.

"What do you think of Moose Manor?" she asked. "Isn't it fun?"

"I love it!" said Ruth Rose.

"It's awesome!" Josh said.

Wallis laughed. "It is something, isn't it? Help me with these groceries, and I'll take you on the grand tour!"

The entrance to the castle turned out to be a regular-sized door around the corner. Wallis and the kids carried bags of groceries into a large room. Dink saw a washer and dryer, wooden pegs for hats and coats, and a pile of sneakers and boots.

"This is my mud room," Wallis said. "The kitchen is through here." She shoved open another door with her hip.

Dink had to tip his head back to see the high ceiling. The usual kitchen stuff was there, with a long wooden table in the middle. A black chandelier hung over the table.

"This place is humongous!" Dink said.

"That's why I love it," Wallis said. "Let's put the food away and I'll show you around."

The kids quickly emptied the bags while Wallis put the milk and ice cream into the refrigerator.

"Okay, the tour begins in the royal

living room," Wallis said. "Follow me!" She led them into the biggest living room Dink had ever seen.

The first thing Dink noticed was the chandelier hanging right over his head. It was as big as Wallis's car!

A marble fireplace took up almost one whole wall. The mantel was dark wood, carved with all kinds of animals.

"This place is amazing!" Dink said.

"Geez," Josh breathed, peering into the fireplace. "You could burn a whole tree in here!"

Wallis flopped onto a pile of floor cushions. "Some winter days I wish I could," she said. "It gets mighty cold up on this cliff."

"How old is this place?" Ruth Rose asked, peering up at the tall stone walls.

"Pretty old," Wallis said. "It was built in the 1930s by a movie star named Emory Scott."

"Awesome!" Josh said.

"What happened to him?" Dink asked.

"Well..." Wallis raised her eyebrows and lowered her voice. "According to the town gossip, he died suddenly. Right here in the castle. In fact, sometimes I think I hear his ghost!"

The kids stared with open mouths.

Then Dink laughed. "Come on, you're just kidding, right?"

"Why? Don't you believe in ghosts?" Wallis asked with a grin.

"No way!" they all yelled.

"Well..." Wallis stood up. "Maybe Emory will introduce himself when he's ready. In the meantime, why don't I show you your rooms?"

The kids grabbed their packs and followed Wallis up a wide stone staircase to the second floor. At the top of the stairs was a dim hallway with several doors.

Wallis pointed to one. "That's my room. Ruth Rose, yours is there, and I've put you boys together, right across the hall."

Wallis tapped on a narrow door at the end of the hall. "This one leads up to the roof."

Dink opened the door to their bedroom. Like the rooms downstairs, the ceiling was high. A blue carpet covered the stone floor. The twin beds had bright red covers.

Dink went to the window and looked outside. All he could see were pine trees. "Where's the ocean?" he asked.

"On the other side," Wallis said. "Why don't you settle in, then come down for lunch?"

Ruth Rose went to her room. Dink and Josh dumped their packs on their beds.

"This place is so cool," Josh said, wandering into their bathroom.

Dink stacked his books on the table next to his bed. He pawed through his clothes, then changed into shorts and a T-shirt.

"Dink, come in here!" Josh called.

Dink wandered into the bathroom.

"Listen," Josh said. He had his ear against one of the bathroom walls.

"What're you doing?" asked Dink.

Josh made a shushing sound. "I thought I heard something!"

"What's going on?" Ruth Rose said as she came into the room.

"Josh thought he heard something behind the wall," Dink said.

Ruth Rose grinned. "It must be the ghost of Emory Scott. He's just waiting for you two to fall asleep tonight!"

Just then they heard Wallis's voice. "Come and get it!" she called. They raced down to the kitchen.

Wallis was packing a basket. "It's such a great day, I thought we'd have a picnic on the beach," she said.

"Cool!" Josh said. "Can we go fishing there sometime?"

Wallis nodded. "Ask Walker if you can borrow some gear. In fact, he's taking you lobstering tomorrow."

"Awesome!" Josh yelled.

Wallis smiled. "You won't think so at four-thirty tomorrow morning."

Dink and Josh each grabbed one end of the picnic basket. Wallis handed Ruth Rose a blanket, then led them to the back of the castle and through another gate.

"Great view, isn't it?" Wallis said. "The first time I saw this place, I knew I had to do my writing here."

Dink took a deep breath of the sea air. Small boats made colorful dots against the blue ocean. "It's really nice," he said.

Josh peered nervously over the cliff. "How do we get down?"

Wallis laughed. "See there? I had steps built. But poor Emory Scott! You remember that marble fireplace and that massive chandelier? Every piece came from Europe by boat. Goodness knows how he got them up this cliff!"

Suddenly a scream burst from the castle behind them.

Dink nearly dropped his end of the picnic basket. The skin on his arms erupted into a thousand goose bumps.

Wallis glanced back and grinned. "Dink, Josh, Ruth Rose, allow me to introduce...the ghost of Emory Scott!"

Chapter 3

The kids stared at Wallis in silence.

She winked at them. "Don't worry, that's just his way of saying hello. Shall we go down?"

The kids glanced at each other, then followed Wallis down the wooden stairs. At the bottom they found a small, sandy beach.

Dink and Josh set the basket in the shade of some boulders while Wallis and Ruth Rose spread the blanket.

"Look! A cave!" Josh said, pointing at a tunnel at the bottom of the cliff. The sea snaked into the dark hole, making a narrow river.

"How far does it go in?" Josh asked, peering into the black space.

"I don't know," Wallis said. "Walker

told me that it's full of bats."

They picnicked on chicken sandwiches, apples, chocolate chip cookies, and cold lemonade. Wallis pointed down the shoreline. "Walker's house is beyond those trees."

"Where is he?" asked Dink.

"Out on his boat," Wallis said, waving a cookie at the ocean. "His lobster pots are scattered over about a half mile of very deep water."

"How does he find them?" Josh asked.

Wallis wiped her fingers on a paper napkin. "Well, he has a good compass aboard *Lady Luck*—that's his boat—and he knows the water."

After their picnic, Wallis put everything back into the basket. "Ready for a walk?"

They hiked along the rocky beach. Ruth Rose poked into tide pools and picked up shells. Josh hung his sneakers around his neck and waded along the shore.

"Better watch out for lobsters," Dink teased. "They like smelly toes."

Josh grinned and splashed Dink.

Rounding a curve in the shoreline, Wallis pointed. "There's Walker's place."

It was a gray cottage with a red roof, surrounded by dune grass and sand.

Just then they heard a shout. Dink looked around and saw someone waving from the end of a dock.

Wallis waved back. "Kids, come and meet our friend Ripley Pearce."

They walked out on the dock toward a long green boat tied at the end. The boat's brass and wood trim gleamed in the sunlight.

A man stood next to the boat, holding a dripping sponge. He had dark slicked-back hair and blue eyes.

"Hi, Rip," Wallis said. "Meet Dink Duncan, Josh Pinto, and Ruth Rose Hathaway."

The man smiled and stuck out a hand. He had dazzling white teeth and a deep tan. "You're fans of this lady's books, right?"

"I've got all of them!" Dink announced.

"I met these three in Connecticut," Wallis explained. "They're spending a week up at the castle. Why don't you come for supper with us tonight?"

"I like your boat," Ruth Rose said. "It's so shiny and clean!"

Rip flashed her a grin. "Thank you very much, little lady. I'll see you tonight at dinner."

Then he looked at Josh. "Want to untie me?" he asked, pointing to a rope tied to the end of the dock.

Josh untied the rope and handed it to Rip.

"Nice meeting you kids," he said, stepping aboard his boat. He started the engine, and the boat pulled smoothly away from the dock.

Dink watched the boat cut through the water. "Maybe I won't be a writer when I grow up. Maybe I'll get a lobster boat."

Wallis grinned at Dink. "Better stick to writing, Dink. Lobsters are getting scarce in Maine."

"I can't wait to go out on Walker's boat," Ruth Rose said.

"My brother's boat is nothing like Rip's," Wallis said. She shook her head. "I don't know how Rip keeps his so clean. Walker's boat looks and smells like a lobster boat."

They walked back toward their picnic spot. Josh kicked water on Ruth

Rose, and she chased him down the beach, yelling all the way.

Dink walked quietly along with Wallis. Overhead, a sea gull cried out.

Dink looked up at Wallis. "Do you really think that scream we heard was the ghost of Emory Scott?"

Wallis laughed. "All I know is I've been hearing those screams since I moved in. The first time, I searched the castle. But I never found a thing."

Dink shivered. "Do you hear the noises a lot?" he asked.

Wallis shrugged. "Sometimes weeks go by and there's not a peep. Then I'll hear them for a few days in a row."

Wallis smiled down at Dink. "To tell you the truth, Dink, this is one mystery that's got me stumped. If those screams aren't the ghost of Emory Scott, I don't know what they are!"

Chapter 4

At the top of the cliff, Wallis took the picnic things. "I need to spend some time working on my new book," she said. "Why don't you guys go exploring? Emory Scott built a playhouse for his kids in those trees. You might want to check it out."

She opened the side door. "Oh, I almost forgot," she said with twinkling eyes. "Some people think his ghost hangs around there, looking for his children. So keep your eyes open!" With that, she went inside.

The kids found a path through the trees. As they walked, Dink told Josh and Ruth Rose what Wallis had said on the beach.

"So it *is* a ghost!" Josh said. "Creepy!"

"No way," Ruth Rose said. "I don't believe in ghosts. It must be an animal trapped somewhere in the castle."

"I don't know," Dink said. "Wallis told me she searched the whole place."

"Besides," said Josh, "what kind of animal makes a spooky scream like that?"

Just then the kids reached the playhouse. The outside of the small wooden building had been painted to look like Wallis's castle. A kid-sized drawbridge crossed a shallow moat to the front door.

"Excellent," said Josh.

"Let's go inside!" Ruth Rose cried, running to the door. She tugged on the handle, and the door opened with a soft whoosh.

Ruth Rose curtsied. "Enter, my loyal knights!"

"His Highness King Dink goes first," Dink said, nudging ahead of Josh.

They crowded into the room. Everything was covered with a layer of dust. Dim light shone through two small windows covered with cobwebs.

Josh rubbed his arms. "Boy, this place is cold," he said.

"Looks like no one's been in here for years," Ruth Rose said.

A round table and two little chairs stood in the middle of the room on a dusty, worn rug. A shelf held a miniature set of blue dishes. Under the shelf, a lonely-looking teddy bear sat on an old sofa.

"This place creeps me out," Josh said.

"Look," Dink said. "Footprints on the rug." He stepped into one of them. "Whoever made these sure has big feet!"

"Do ghosts leave footprints?" Josh asked.

"Maybe it's Walker," Ruth Rose suggested. "They're too big to be Wallis's."

"But why would Walker come here?" Dink wondered out loud.

"Can we go?" Josh pleaded. "I just saw a monster spider, and he was looking back at me!"

"Okay, but let's come back," Ruth Rose said. "I want to clean this place. It's sad to see it all dusty like this."

Ruth Rose pulled the door shut behind them. As they crossed the drawbridge, Dink noticed something in the moat. He jumped down and picked up a bright green feather.

"Hey, guys, look! It's like the one that was stuck to Josh's sneaker."

Ruth Rose held the feather up to the sun. "What's it from?"

Josh examined the feather. "The only bird I know with this kind of feather is a parrot," he said. "But parrots don't live in Maine."

Dink took the feather back from

Josh, then put it in his pocket.

"Okay, we've explored the play-house," Josh said. "Now you guys have to do what I want."

Dink grinned at his friend. "You mean eat?"

"No. I want to check out that cave down on the beach."

"Wait a minute," Dink said. "You were creeped out by the playhouse, but you want to explore the cave?"

"Caves are cool," Josh said. "Come on, you guys."

The kids headed past the castle, through the gate, and down the cliff. They stood looking at the small river flowing out of the cave. "I wonder how deep it is," Dink said.

"There's one way to find out," Josh said. He stepped in the water and began wading into the cave. The water reached just above his ankles.

"Come on, you guys!" he called over his shoulder.

Dink and Ruth Rose followed him. The cave grew darker, until the sunlight disappeared. The air was cold and damp, and the black walls felt slimy.

"Josh, this water is freezing," Ruth Rose said. Her voice sounded hollow. "I hate it in here! Can we go back?"

"The water's getting deeper, too," Dink said. "And I can't even see you guys!"

"Shh!" Josh said. "I heard something!"

"Josh, don't try to scare us!" Ruth Rose said. "I'm already—"

Suddenly a scream echoed through the cave.

"RUN!" Ruth Rose yelled.

Over their heads, hundreds of black bats streaked for daylight.

Chapter 5

The kids didn't stop running till they were at the top of the cliff. Dink threw himself on the ground, trying to catch his breath.

"What was that?" Ruth Rose asked, pulling off her sopping sneakers. "My heart nearly stopped!"

"It was the ghost!" Josh said. "I bet that cave leads to a secret dungeon under the castle. Maybe that's where Emory Scott died!"

Ruth Rose burst out laughing. Josh ignored her. "There must be a secret

door leading to the dungeon somewhere. And I'm going to find it!"

"Maybe you are," Dink said. "But
I'm gonna take a shower and change."

"Me too," Ruth Rose said. "I smell
like a fish!"

When they got back to the castle,
Walker's Jeep was parked out front.
The kids cleaned up, then hurried
down to the kitchen. Wallis, Walker,
and Rip were sitting at the long table,
husking ears of corn.

"Hi, kids," Walker said. "How was
your first day at Moose Manor?"

"It was great," Josh said, shooting
Dink a look. "We explored the play-

house and found some neat stuff on the beach."

Dink figured Josh wanted to keep his "secret dungeon" idea to himself.

"Well, I have lobsters to cook," Wallis said. "I hope everyone's hungry!"

After supper, the grownups decided to play Scrabble.

"You kids can join us," Wallis said. "Or you can choose another board game from the hall closet. Help yourself."

"Um...I think I'll go upstairs and read," Josh said. He motioned for Dink and Ruth Rose to follow him. They met upstairs in the hall between the bedrooms. "Let's search up here while they're playing Scrabble," he said.

"What exactly are we looking for?" Dink asked.

"A secret door or passageway," Josh

said, rapping his knuckle lightly on a wall.

"Josh, don't you think Wallis would've told us about a secret door?" Ruth Rose said.

"Maybe she doesn't know about it," Josh said.

"I guess we should look around," Dink agreed. "*Something* is making those weird noises."

"Let's start on the roof," Ruth Rose said.

They walked down the hall, and Josh pushed open the narrow door.

At the top of the stairs, they opened another door. A cool breeze blew in their faces as they stepped onto the flat roof.

"Wow! You can see everything!" said Josh. "It would be neat to fly a kite up here!"

Dink stood between two granite

battlements that were taller than he was. He felt like a king looking over his land.

"There's nothing up here," Josh said.

"Okay," Dink said. "Let's look downstairs."

The kids tromped back down to the hall.

Ruth Rose walked into her room while Dink and Josh searched theirs. Dink started with the closet, but found only dust and an old tennis racket.

He used the racket to poke behind the window curtains. A few spiders darted away, but nothing else.

Suddenly Josh screamed from the bathroom. "Dink, it's got me! Help!"

Dink charged into the bathroom, holding the tennis racket like a club. He looked around wildly, but the room was empty.

"Josh? Where are you?"

The shower curtain flew open. Josh stood there, grinning. "Boo!"

Dink shook his head. "You're so lame, Josh. It would serve you right if some ghost did get you!"

Josh climbed out of the tub. "Thought you didn't believe in ghosts, Dinkus!"

Dink just shook his head again. He crossed the hall and knocked on Ruth Rose's door. "Find anything?" he asked.

She shook her head. "Nope."

She and Dink searched the long hall. They looked behind the radiators and inside plant pots and one tall umbrella stand.

Josh tapped on the walls, listening for hollow sounds. Finally they gave up, sweaty and dusty.

"I don't know where else to search," Dink said.

"We didn't check out the downstairs rooms," Josh said.

"We'll have to wait till tomorrow," Ruth Rose said, yawning. "I'm going to bed. And I hope I don't dream about ghosts, thanks to Josh Pinto!"

Josh grinned. "I read somewhere that ghosts eat girls with curls."

"Just let one try!" she said, then slammed her door.

Dink and Josh climbed into bed. A few minutes later they were both asleep.

Dink woke suddenly, his heart thumping. He looked at the clock. It was midnight!

Dink climbed out of bed and tiptoed to the window. He saw black trees against a blacker sky.

Then he saw it—a ghostly light near the playhouse!

Chapter 6

Dink gulped and felt goose bumps climbing his legs. Could it be Emory Scott's ghost?

The light winked a few more times, then disappeared.

Dink shivered, rubbing his eyes. When the light didn't return, he crawled back into bed.

He yawned and closed his eyes, deciding that he had seen a firefly.

But just before falling off to sleep, Dink opened his eyes again. He had seen only one light moving out there in the darkness.

Why would there be only one firefly in the woods? He thought about that until he fell asleep.

Dink dreamed that he was in the cave again. It was pitch dark. Up ahead, he heard a hideous scream. But this time, the scream didn't stop, it just got louder. Suddenly bats were flying in his face. But these bats had feathers—bright green feathers!

Dink bolted upright in his bed. The blankets were twisted around his legs and the alarm clock was buzzing.

I'm not in a cave, Dink realized. I'm still in the castle. Relieved, he shut off the alarm.

"Josh, wake up," he said.

Josh opened an eye. "Why?"

Dink climbed out of bed. "Walker's taking us lobstering, remember?" He turned on the light and yanked Josh's covers off.

"Come on, let's go catch a lobster!"

Josh groaned, but he climbed out of bed. "I hate lobsters."

Dink laughed. "You ate one last night." He pulled on yesterday's jeans and a warm sweatshirt over his T-shirt. "I'm going downstairs. Don't go back to bed!"

Dink crossed the hall and tapped on Ruth Rose's door. She was up and dressed in yellow from top to bottom.

"Did you see anything strange last night?" Dink asked.

Ruth Rose was pulling a brush through her hair. She shook her head.

"Well, I did! I'll tell you about it downstairs."

There was a light on in the kitchen. Dink saw juice glasses, cereal bowls, and some muffins on the table. He was munching when Ruth Rose and Josh came in.

"Guys, I think someone was creeping around outside last night," Dink said. He told them about the light he'd seen in the woods.

Josh grabbed a muffin and bit off half.

"Told you," he said, trying to grin and chew at the same time. "It was Emory's ghost!"

"Very funny, Josh," Ruth Rose said.

Just then there was a thump in the mud room and the kitchen door crashed open. Josh nearly fell out of his chair.

Walker came in wearing tall rubber boots and a yellow slicker. "Ready to go?" he asked.

Dink laughed in relief. "Josh thought you were a ghost," he said.

"Did not," Josh muttered.

They walked outside and climbed into Walker's Jeep. The sky was pitch black. Dink peered into the woods, half expecting to see the strange light again.

A few minutes later Walker turned into his driveway. They got out and walked behind the house to the dock. Their feet made hollow noises on the wooden boards.

"Watch your step out here," Walker said, aiming a flashlight at Dink's feet.

Dink breathed in the salty night air. A few stars made pinpoints of light above the boat. Somewhere, he heard a night bird call.

"Ready to come aboard?" Walker asked.

Dink, Josh, and Ruth Rose followed Walker onto the dark boat.

Chapter 7

"Better slip one of those on," Walker said when they were aboard. He pointed at orange life jackets hanging on a row of pegs.

The kids climbed into the bulky vests and sat on benches. Walker started the motor, and the small boat moved away from the dock.

"It'll be about an hour before we get to my pots," Walker hollered over the roar of the engine. "Get comfortable!"

Ruth Rose and Josh curled up on the benches, but Dink sat up. He didn't